D0516466

by Anna Kang *illustrated by* Christopher Weyant

I Am (Not) Scared

two lions

To Holly McGhee, for your faith and friendship

Published by Two Lions, New York
www.apub.com

ISBN-13: 9781503937451 (hardcover)
ISBN-10: 1503937453 (hardcover)

Design by Abby Dening

The illustrations are rendered in ink and watercolor with brush pens on Arches paper.

Printed in China
First edition
1 3 5 7 9 10 8 6 4 2

You are scared.

I am not scared. . . .

Are *you*?

No, I am brave.
This will be fun!

You look scared.

LOOP OF
Well, maybe a little.
Don't worry,
there are *much* scarier
things than *this*.

DOOM

Like *what*?
Like . . .
snakes!

Snakes?
Yes. They are scary!

Or what
about a tub
of hairy
spiders?

Now *that*
is scary.

A pan of
fried ants!
Or a pit of
hot lava!

An alien
with pink
eyes and
furry teeth!

A ROLLER COASTER!

With
a SNAKE!

WHOOSH

Let’s be
scared
together.

AAAAAA
VRO

AHHH!!!!
OOOOOWWWW

I AM

SCARED!

Now THAT was scary.

WE ARE SCARED!!!